HUMPHREY CARPENTER

Mr Majeika and the Ghost Train

Illustrated by Frank Rodgers

PUFFIN

Contents

PUFFIN BOOKS

Published by the Penguin Group
Penguin Books Ltd, 80 Strand, London WC2R 0RL, England
Penguin Group (USA) Inc., 375 Hudson Street, New York, New York 10014, USA
Penguin Group (Canada), 90 Eglinton Avenue East, Suite 700, Toronto, Ontario, Canada M4P 2Y3
(a division of Pearson Penguin Canada Inc.)
Penguin Ireland, 25 St Stephen's Green, Dublin 2, Ireland (a division of Penguin Books Ltd)
Penguin Group (Australia), 250 Camberwell Road, Camberwell, Victoria 3124, Australia
(a division of Pearson Australia Group Pty Ltd)
Penguin Books India Pvt Ltd, 11 Community Centre, Panchsheel Park, New Delhi – 110 017, India
Penguin Group (NZ), 67 Apollo Drive, Rosedale, North Shore 0632, New Zealand
(a division of Pearson New Zealand Ltd)
Penguin Books (South Africa) (Pty) Ltd, 24 Sturdee Avenue, Rosebank, Johannesburg 2196, South Africa

Penguin Books Ltd, Registered Offices: 80 Strand, London WC2R 0RL, England

puffinbooks.com

First published by Viking 1994
Published in Puffin Books 1995
This edition published 2010 for The Book People Ltd,
Hall Wood Avenue, Haydock, St Helens WA11 9UL
001 – 10 9 8 7 6 5 4 3 2 1

Text copyright © Humphrey Carpenter, 1994
Illustrations copyright © Frank Rodgers, 1994
All rights reserved

The moral right of the author and illustrator has been asserted

Set in Palatino

Printed in Great Britain by Clays Ltd, St Ives plc

British Library Cataloguing in Publication Data
A CIP catalogue record for this book is available from the British Library

ISBN: 978-0-141-33688-6

www.greenpenguin.co.uk

Penguin Books is committed to a sustainable future
for our business, our readers and our planet.
The book in your hands is made from paper
certified by the Forest Stewardship Council.

1. *Hamish gets a letter*

Somebody had stuck a poster on the wall just outside St Barty's School:

Opening next week
ADVENTURE GALAXY
The most exciting theme park in Britain!
Fairy-tale Castles – Space Rides
Roller-coasters – Haunted Houses
Don't wait to come and try it!!

Most of Class Three were gathered round the poster. 'That looks exciting,' said Jody.

'You bet,' said Thomas. 'Pete and I went to an adventure park for our birthday treat.' (Thomas and Pete were twins.) 'It was the best day of our lives.'

'The rides were absolutely fabulous,'

agreed Pete. 'There was a thing called the Giant Catapult, which shot you right up into the sky. It was really neat. I loved it.'

'No you didn't,' said Thomas. 'You were sick all over me.'

'And *you* were terrified in the Haunted House,' said Pete.

'Those Haunted Houses are boring,' said Jody. 'Just people dressed up as skeletons, jumping out at you and shouting "Boo!"'

'This one was different,' explained Thomas. 'It was all done with lasers, and there were really horrid shapes coming at you out of the walls, making screeching noises.'

'You were so frightened you shut your eyes and stuck your fingers in your ears,' said Pete.

'No I didn't,' said Thomas, and they began to have a fight about it, which was only stopped by the bell ringing for the start of school.

When they got to their classroom, Mr Majeika was there, waiting to take the register. Mr Majeika had once been a wizard, and sometimes strange things happened when he was teaching Class

Three. But most of the time he had to do the same boring things as other teachers, like taking the register, and getting cross with people who were late or badly behaved.

This morning, Hamish Bigmore was late. Mr Majeika didn't seem to be cross about this. 'I think he likes it when Hamish is late,' Jody whispered to Pete, 'because then he doesn't have to put up with Hamish being rude to him, and causing trouble all the time.'

'Now, everyone,' said Mr Majeika, when he had finished the register, 'I've got a letter here, from the people who are opening the new Adventure Galaxy theme park, just down the road. They say that anyone who wants to can have a free ticket for the opening day.'

Class Three cheered, and everyone said they would like tickets, so Mr

Majeika began to hand them out. It was now that Hamish Bigmore walked through the door.

He had a pocket computer game in his hand. It was playing loud music, and was making bleeping noises, and Hamish didn't take his eyes off it even for a moment, as he walked to his place and sat down.

'Hamish,' warned Mr Majeika, 'put that thing away at once.' Hamish Bigmore didn't even bother to answer; he just went on playing the computer game. 'If you won't do what I say,' said Mr Majeika, growing very angry, 'I shall have to – have to – '

The trouble was, he didn't know what. During his first term teaching Class Three, Mr Majeika had turned Hamish into a frog, and it had been very hard to turn him back again. Since then, he had tried other magical punishments for Hamish's bad behaviour, but each time they had gone wrong.

'I'll tell you what you can do, Mr Majeika,' said Hamish, grinning – and still playing his computer game while he talked. 'You can send me into this game, so I can really play it myself, and not just press buttons. How about that?'

Mr Majeika shook his head. It was just the sort of thing he found himself doing, when he muttered a spell over Hamish without stopping to think. He could imagine all the bother there would be if Hamish got into the computer game. There would have to be spells to fetch him out again, and probably they would bring all the creatures and things in the computer game out into the classroom too, and it would be ages before everything was back to normal.

'No, I've got a better idea,' said Mr Majeika. 'If you don't put that thing down at once, Hamish, I won't let you have your free ticket for the opening of Adventure Galaxy.'

Hamish seemed to be so surprised that he *did* stop playing the computer game. 'Adventure Galaxy?' he said, his mouth dropping open. 'You must be joking, Mr

Majeika. You don't really think *I* want to go to that playground for little babies?'

'It isn't for babies, Hamish,' said Jody. 'It sounds very exciting.'

'You think it's *exciting*, do you?' sneered Hamish at Jody. 'Likkle baby Jody likes fairy-tale castles, does she? And likkle pretend haunted houses, where likkle pretend ghosties say boo to her? All right, likkle Jody, you go off to likkle Adventure Galaxy, and leave me here with something a bit more grown up.' He started playing the computer game again.

Mr Majeika was getting so angry that he knew in a moment he'd lose his temper, and there *would* be a spell, whether he meant to do it or not. Fortunately, just then, the classroom door opened.

It was Mr Potter, the head teacher of St

Barty's, and he was holding an envelope.
'Excuse me, Mr Majeika,' he said, 'but I
have a letter here for Hamish Bigmore.
It's marked "Urgent", so I thought I'd
bring it in at once.' He gave it to Hamish,
and went away again.

Hamish stopped playing the computer

game, and opened the envelope. 'Who's it from, Hamish?' called Thomas.

'Perhaps it's a love letter from his girl-friend,' giggled Pete.

'Hamish hasn't got a girl-friend,' said Jody, 'except Wilhelmina Worlock.'

Everyone laughed. Wilhelmina Worlock was a witch who sometimes turned up at St Barty's School, and made a dreadful nuisance of herself. The only person who liked her was Hamish.

Hamish didn't reply; he put the letter in his pocket, switched off his computer game, and said to Mr Majeika: 'I'd like to come to Adventure Galaxy, after all, please.'

Nobody had *ever* heard Hamish say 'please' before. Mr Majeika was so surprised that he stopped being angry, and gave him a ticket. Hamish Bigmore behaved himself for the rest of the day, while Mr Majeika got on with teaching Class Three.

After school was over, Jody hurried up to Thomas and Pete. 'You know my joke about Hamish and Wilhelmina?' she said. 'Well, I was right. Hamish left the envelope on the floor, and it was addressed in *her* handwriting!'

2. *All aboard*

On the day of the free visit to Adventure Galaxy, Class Three arrived at the theme park early in the morning, even before the gates had opened. Mr Majeika was with them. 'It was nice of Mr Potter to say we could do it as a school trip,' he said, 'but I don't think there's anything very educational about this place.' He was looking doubtfully at the enormous rides they could see through the gates.

'There's one thing you'll have to learn, Mr Majeika,' said Jody. 'Not to be sick when you get whizzed right up in the air, and then whizzed down again.'

'I don't think I'll be very good at that,' said Mr Majeika. 'We used to have a game we played when I was a wizard. Each of us sat on a broomstick and

16

whizzed through the air, and we tried to knock each other off. I always felt terribly sick.'

'It sounds like the Dodgem Cars,' said Pete, as the gates opened. 'Come on, Mr Majeika, let's see what you're like driving a Dodgem.'

But when Mr Majeika saw the Dodgem Cars, he said they were too frightening,

and wouldn't go on them. 'That looks much nicer,' he said, pointing at an old-fashioned roundabout, on which painted wooden horses were moving up and down at quite a gentle speed, while an organ played jolly music.

'That's just baby stuff, Mr Majeika,' said Thomas. 'Come on, we'll take you on some really exciting rides.'

Melanie, who was always finding something to cry about, burst into tears. 'I want to go on the galloping horses!' she wept.

'All right, go on them, then,' said Pete, 'but don't expect us to come with you.'

Melanie sobbed even louder. 'I'm too frightened to go by myself!' she howled.

'I'll come with you, Melanie,' said Mr Majeika, and the two of them climbed on to one of the galloping horses. The music began, the horse moved, and the

roundabout turned faster and faster. It
was very exciting. When it stopped, Mr
Majeika felt quite giddy.

'Oh, that was wonderful!' cried
Melanie. 'I wish I could gallop away on
this lovely horse.'

'What a good idea,' said Mr Majeika,

19

who wasn't thinking properly on account of feeling giddy. He muttered a spell, and in a moment the wooden horse had come to life. With Mr Majeika and Melanie still on its back, it leapt off the roundabout and galloped across Adventure Galaxy, weaving between the rides and the stalls selling sweets and refreshments. Since it was still quite early in the morning, there were very few people about. Mr Majeika quickly came to his senses, and realized that there would be awful trouble if he and Melanie stole one of the horses. So he made it go back on to the roundabout, and said a spell to turn it back to wood again. The man in charge of the roundabout (who had been counting money in his little office) hadn't noticed anything odd.

Of course, everyone in Class Three wanted a ride – a real ride – on a roundabout horse too, and they were very sad when Mr Majeika said no. The only person who didn't seem interested was Hamish Bigmore. He kept looking around him, as if he was trying to find something.

'What's up with Hamish?' Thomas asked Jody.

'I don't know,' said Jody. 'I bet it's something to do with that letter he had from Wilhelmina Worlock. That's why he wanted to come here. But I don't see any sign of Miss Worlock, do you?'

'No,' said Pete, 'thank goodness. We've seen enough of that dreadful old hag to last a lifetime.'

Class Three walked through Adventure Galaxy looking at the other rides, but after the magical happening with the horse, everything seemed rather dull. Suddenly, Hamish got excited and began shouting: 'There it is!' he cried. 'The Ghost Train!'

Sure enough, a big sign over one of the rides said GHOST TRAIN in spooky writing. But it was rather a little train, and when Thomas and Pete peered behind the ride, there didn't seem to be anywhere for it to go. 'The really good Ghost Trains run on a very long track,' said Pete. 'But this one is tiny.'

'Anyway,' said Thomas, 'it'll only be people dressed up as ghosts, shouting "Boo". It doesn't say anything about lasers, or exciting things like that. Let's go and see if there's a Giant Catapult. That'll be much more exciting.'

'Oh no, we *must* go on this,' said Hamish anxiously.

'*Must*, Hamish?' asked Mr Majeika suspiciously. 'Why must we? Are you up to something?'

Hamish shook his head hastily. 'Oh no, Mr Majeika,' he said. 'I just thought everyone would enjoy it.'

'He *is* up to something,' Pete whispered to Thomas. 'But I can't think what. He's probably got some friends hiding in there, who are going to throw buckets of goo over us, or something silly.'

'You know Hamish hasn't got any friends,' whispered Thomas. 'But I'm sure he's got some trick up his sleeve.' He turned to Mr Majeika.

'Do be careful, Mr Majeika,' he said. 'There might be real ghosts in there.'

'That would be fine,' said Mr Majeika. 'I know lots of ghosts, or at least I used to when I was a wizard, and they're mostly frightfully nice. Come on!'

There was no one in charge of the Ghost Train, but a notice said: *Please take your seats, dearies, and the train will move when the bell rings.*

'"Dearies" is a bit odd,' said Jody. 'It sounds the sort of thing Wilhelmina Worlock would say.'

Just at that moment, the bell rang. 'Quick, everyone!' called Hamish, and they all climbed aboard – all except Melanie.

24

'I'm frightened!' she sobbed. 'Jody,
please look after me.'

Jody sighed, and got off the train
again. 'Come on, Melanie,' she said,
'we'll go and buy you a nice teddy bear
balloon. See you all in five minutes!' she
called to Class Three.

Off went Jody and Melanie, and the
train started to move. Suddenly, Hamish
Bigmore jumped off it. 'Just remembered

something I had to go and do!' he called to Mr Majeika and Class Three. 'Goodbye, everyone! And I really mean *goodbye*!' He began to laugh a very nasty laugh.

It took Jody and Melanie a little while to find a stall selling teddy bear balloons. They bought one, and came back to the Ghost Train.

Except that the Ghost Train just wasn't there. Where it had been standing, there was just an empty space.

'Oh dear,' said Jody. 'I don't like the look of this.'

Melanie burst into tears again.

3. *Jody turns detective*

'There's no point in crying,' said Jody. 'I expect the Ghost Train has been moved to some other part of Adventure Galaxy. We'll just have to go and look.'

So they went and looked. But there was no sign of the Ghost Train, and the more she thought about it, the more Jody reckoned it would have been impossible to move it in just a few minutes. It was very strange.

'There's Hamish!' sobbed Melanie. 'I bet horrid Hamish has something to do with it.'

Hamish was wandering around with his hands in his pockets, looking pleased with himself.

'What's happened to the Ghost Train?' Jody called to him. 'Where's

Mr Majeika and Class Three?'

Hamish grinned. 'They've just gone on a much longer journey than they expected,' he said, laughing nastily.

Jody grabbed hold of Hamish's arm. 'What have you been up to?' she said angrily. 'What have you done with them? When will they be back again?'

'I don't know anything about it,' said Hamish, trying to stamp on Jody's toes.

'You just said you did!' shouted Jody. 'You said they'd gone on a long journey. When will they be back?'

'I don't know if they will be,' sneered Hamish nastily. 'A friend of mine is looking after them for a bit, and if you're nasty to me, she may never send them back at all!'

'I can guess who that is,' said Jody, trying to twist Hamish's arm. 'You had a letter from Wilhelmina Worlock.

She's behind this, isn't she?'

'It wasn't a letter, it was just a Christmas card,' said Hamish, who was obviously lying, since it wasn't Christmas. 'Let go of me, or I'll turn my Death Ray Gun on you.' He took a plastic gun out of his pocket and waved

it nastily in Jody's face. Melanie started to cry louder than ever.

'Don't worry, Melanie,' said Jody, 'it's only a toy out of a cereal packet. But we're wasting our time with Hamish. Let's go back to school, and see if Mr Majeika and everyone else has managed to get back by another way.'

Jody and Melanie walked back to school, and by the time they got there, it was half way through the lunch break. Mr Potter was standing anxiously at the gate, looking at his watch. 'Ah, there you are at last,' he said. 'We were keeping dinner for you, but the food is getting cold.'

'Isn't the rest of Class Three back yet, Mr Potter?' asked Jody. Mr Potter shook his head. 'That's very worrying,' said Jody. She was going to tell Mr Potter what had happened, then she began to think what he might do about it. He'd call the police, and they would search Adventure Galaxy and ask Hamish lots of questions, and probably they wouldn't discover anything at all. The police weren't going to believe that a wicked, magical witch had spirited away an entire class of children and their teacher. Jody decided to say nothing to Mr Potter. She would have to be a detective herself.

'I expect they've all got held up in one of the queues for the rides at Adventure Galaxy,' she said to Mr Potter. 'I'll leave Melanie here, so she can have her dinner, and I'll go back and tell them all to hurry up.' Without stopping to ask Mr Potter if this was all right, Jody hurried off again, leaving Melanie to have her lunch.

When she got back to Adventure Galaxy, she saw Hamish sitting at a table outside one of the refreshment stalls,

drinking a large coke. He seemed to be
rather cross, and kept looking at his
watch. Jody crept up and hid herself
behind a large rubbish bin that was next
to Hamish's chair.

'Well, if it isn't my Star Pupil,' she
hissed loudly in a voice that was meant
to sound like Wilhelmina Worlock.

Hamish jumped with surprise, then looked all around him. 'About time too,' he said. 'I've been waiting for you for ages. Where are you? I can't see you.'

'I've decided to be invisible, my little Star Pupil,' hissed Jody in the Wilhelmina voice. Miss Worlock had called Hamish her Star Pupil when she first came to St Barty's and tried to take over the school. He was the only person there horrid enough for her to like. 'Yes, I'm invisible, because I'm not here at all. I'm somewhere else – with *them*.'

'What are you doing with them?' said Hamish eagerly. 'Are you putting spiders down their clothes, and making ghosts jump out at them, and frightening them so their hair turns white?'

'Much horrider things than that, my Star Pupil,' hissed Jody. 'Aren't you going to come and see?'

'Of course I am,' said Hamish crossly.
'You said in your letter that I could come
and watch you being horrid to them.
And I've been waiting here for more than
an hour.'

'Come along, then,' hissed Jody. 'I'll
see you shortly. Bye-bye!'

'But where do I go?' asked Hamish
angrily. 'How do I get to where you've
taken them?'

This was what Jody had wanted to find
out: whether Hamish knew where the
Ghost Train had gone. As he didn't, she
would have to start looking for it herself.

She crept away from Hamish, and
went back to where the Ghost Train had
been standing. This time she saw
something she hadn't noticed before. In
the middle of the open space, flat in the
ground, was an iron manhole cover. On
it were stamped the letters 'W.W.'.

The manhole cover had a handle, but when Jody tried to lift it, it was far too heavy. She hurried back to the café, where Hamish was finishing his coke. Jody decided not to pretend to be Wilhelmina again. She went straight up to Hamish and said: 'I know where the Ghost Train has gone. Come and see.'

Hamish looked very cross, but he followed her, and when they got to the manhole cover, he said: 'Why didn't the silly old bag tell me?'

'So, you do admit you were in the plot with Wilhelmina!' said Jody. 'Help me lift it.'

'No way,' said Hamish.

'In that case,' said Jody, 'you'll never get down there and see what's going on. If we try together we can do it.'

Hamish grumbled, but he helped Jody to try to lift it, and after a moment they

managed to move the manhole cover. It
opened to show a sinister-looking
staircase winding down into the
darkness. A distant roaring noise could
be heard.

'Come on,' said Jody. 'We're going
down.'

Hamish looked thoroughly frightened,
but when Jody started down the stairs,
he followed her.

4. *Where the weather comes from*

'Hamish has jumped off!' called Thomas to Mr Majeika, as the Ghost Train started to move. 'He's up to some trick!'

It was too late for Mr Majeika to do anything. The train had begun to whizz round and round in a circle, at a tremendous speed, as if it was being sucked into a whirlpool. A moment later, that was exactly what happened – it disappeared with a *whoosh*, through a hole which had suddenly opened up in the ground.

Everything went very black, and Thomas and Pete wondered if they would ever see daylight again. They were travelling at a tremendous speed. 'This is even faster than the Giant

Catapult,' called out Pete, but Thomas was feeling too sick to say anything.

Suddenly the train slowed down, and it began to get light again. Soon, they were travelling at an ordinary speed through grey misty countryside. The railway line on which they were running was overhung with trees which brushed

damp branches against them as they passed.

'It's not like any Ghost Train I've ever been on,' called Thomas. 'Where do you think we are, Mr Majeika?'

Mr Majeika scratched his head. 'I'm not sure,' he said, 'but I think I've been here before, about four hundred years ago, when I was quite a young wizard. It's gradually coming back to me.'

Suddenly the train stopped, in the middle of nowhere. 'Let me think!' said Mr Majeika excitedly. 'Yes, this is the Ghost Station!' He muttered some words, and alongside the line the ghostly shape of a railway station began to appear.

There were ghostly people on the platform too. Thomas and Pete could recognize several people from history, including Julius Caesar, Napoleon, and several sad-looking men and women who were carrying their heads underneath their arms. When they saw the train, they tried to climb aboard.

'The nine fifty is late again,' grumbled Julius Caesar. 'I haven't got to the office on time any day this week.'

'And it's completely full,' said Napoleon crossly, peering at the seats where Thomas and Pete were sitting. 'It's quite unfair to us season-ticket holders.'

'We are not amused,' said a woman whom Thomas recognized as Queen Victoria. 'Shove over, do.'

'Where are you all trying to get to?' asked Pete.

'We can make some room for them, Mr Majeika,' said Thomas. 'There's space for one of them on each of the seats.'

'Don't do that, for goodness sake,' said Mr Majeika anxiously. 'Don't even talk to

them. If you have anything to do with a
ghost for more than just a few moments,
you'll turn into a ghost yourself. Ah,
that's better, the train is moving again.'

They rolled off along the track, leaving
the famous ghosts shouting angrily.
Thomas even thought he saw Queen

Victoria running down the line after them, waving an umbrella. Mr Majeika hurriedly said another spell, and the ghosts and their station vanished again.

'Poor things,' said Pandora Green, who was sitting next to Mr Majeika. 'I hope another train turns up, so they can catch it.'

'It won't,' said Mr Majeika. 'They're always on that platform, waiting and waiting. Mind you, most of them kept other people waiting when they were alive, so perhaps it serves them right. Now, we seem to be arriving somewhere.'

'And the weather's getting worse,' said Pete, because it had begun to rain heavily – and also, which was odd, to snow and hail at the same time.

'Yes, but it's quite sunny too,' said Pandora, pointing at a big patch of sunlight to the left of the train. 'And look, there's a rainbow.'

'And lightning too,' said Thomas. 'How very strange.'

'Not at all,' said Mr Majeika. 'I know where we are. This is the Weather Factory.'

'The what, Mr Majeika?' they all asked him.

'The place where the weather is made. Why are you all staring? It has to be made somewhere, doesn't it?' The train came to a halt, and Mr Majeika got out. 'Come on, everyone, let's go and see who's running the Weather Factory these days.'

The Weather Factory was a big tall building, built of something grey that looked like solid cloud. All kinds of pipes and turrets, and funnels and nozzles were sticking out of it, and from these

were coming the rain, snow, hail,
lightning and rainbows that they had
seen. A large door had a stern notice on
it: WEATHER WORKERS ONLY.
WELLINGTON BOOTS MUST BE
WORN.

'In we go,' said Mr Majeika cheerily.

'But we haven't got any wellies,' said Pandora.

'That's easy,' said Mr Majeika, shutting his eyes and waving his arms. In a moment, all of Class Three found their shoes had turned into lovely new shiny wellington boots.

Inside the Weather Factory, there was a great deal of noise – a roaring and hissing, and banging and fizzling – and it was quite some time before Class Three could see who was working all the machines, on account of all the clouds and other kinds of weather that were filling the air. At last, they spotted a very old man with a long white beard, who was rushing about from one machine to another, looking dreadfully cross and fed up. He was staring at a piece of paper in his hand. 'Now, let me see,' he muttered, 'it says snow for Scotland

here, but I haven't got any snow left –
it's all been used up in Iceland – so it'll
have to be hailstones.' He hurried over to
a machine and pulled a handle. There
was a loud bang which made him jump.
'Bother,' he said, 'wrong lever. That
means thunder in Paris, which wasn't
what they were expecting at all. I shall be
in trouble again!' At this moment he saw

Mr Majeika and Class Three. His face lit up at once, and he smiled the broadest of smiles.

'Ah!' he cried. 'How wonderful! Someone to take over from me at last. And lots and lots of you, so you'll manage the job easily.'

'I'm afraid we haven't come to do your job,' said Mr Majeika. 'We're here because we were brought by a Ghost Train that got out of control. But we'd like to have a look around.'

'What's that piece of paper?' asked Pandora.

'It's the weather forecasts for the whole world,' said the weather man. 'You know how, in the newspaper and on television, it tells you what the weather's going to be? Well, they send me a copy, and then I have to make sure it's exactly what they've forecast. Only

I'm so busy I often make a mistake,' he ended gloomily.

'Which is why the forecasts are often wrong,' said Thomas. 'I understand now. But how did you come to be a weather man? What were you before?'

'I was once a schoolmaster,' said the weather man, wiping a tired hand across his forehead. 'I was foolish enough to answer an advertisement for this job. Teaching was hard work, but this is worse. I really don't think I can go on much longer.'

'Don't worry, dearie, you won't have to, tee hee!' cackled a voice that Class Three all knew horribly well. It was, of course, Wilhelmina Worlock.

She had stuck her head round the door of the Weather Factory. 'Hello, Wilhelmina,' said Mr Majeika wearily. 'So, what are you up to this time?'

'Perfectly simple,' snarled Miss Worlock. 'Our friend here, the weather man, can go back to being a silly teacher. And you lot are taking over his job – for ever and ever and ever! You can say goodbye to St blooming Barty's School, and your cosy little homes. You won't be seeing them again!'

5. *Poor old Dennis*

'Hamish Bigmore, you're a coward,' Jody called out. She had walked down about a hundred steps into the darkness. Hamish was a long way behind her, coming down the staircase very slowly.

'No I'm n-n-not,' came Hamish's voice. 'B-b-but I've left something b-b-behind. I need to go back.'

'The only thing you've left behind is your courage,' called Jody. 'Come on!'

The roaring noise was getting louder. By the time Jody had gone down fifty more steps, it became deafening. Suddenly the staircase ended, and Jody found herself out in daylight – at least there was some sort of light, though she couldn't see the sun, and guessed that she must be in some huge underground cave, which was somehow lit from above. In front of her was a large cage. And in the cage was an enormous dragon.

Jody knew it was a dragon, because it was red and scaly, and it had an enormous tail and huge wings. But its wings were feebly crumpled up, and looked as if they hadn't been used for a long time. Its eyes were shut, and there

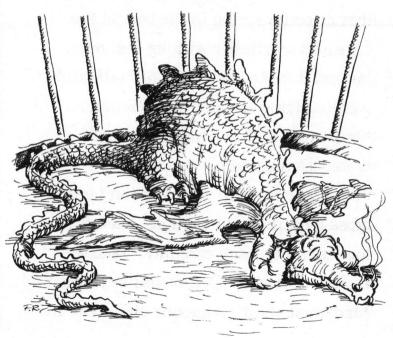

was no fire, just a little steam and smoke coming out of its nostrils. It was roaring sadly to itself in its sleep.

Jody watched it for a moment, but from as close as this the roaring was deafening, and, without thinking what she was doing, Jody rattled the bars of the cage and shouted: 'Oh, do shut up!'

The dragon jumped, opened both its eyes, and stared at her. Jody felt terrified that it would spring to the bars of the cage and scorch her with its fire, but instead it looked ashamed of itself, and went on lying where it was. 'Sorry, Madam,' it said in a humble tone of voice. 'Dennis didn't mean to disturb you, really he didn't. Please don't get cross with poor old Dennis.' Then it looked at her more carefully. 'Wait a moment,' it said, 'Dennis thinks this isn't Madam at all. It's someone else. Who has

come down the staircase to look at poor
old Dennis through the bars of his cage?'

'My name is Jody,' said Jody, 'and I'm
looking for the rest of my class from
school, and our teacher, Mr Majeika.'

'Majeika?' said the dragon in a
thoughtful voice. 'Dennis is sure he's
heard that name somewhere before. He

thinks there was once a wizard called Majeika, who got into trouble, and was sent away, or maybe locked up in a cage, like poor old Dennis.'

'That's the one!' said Jody. 'They made him become a teacher. Have you seen him, and have you seen a Ghost Train go past?'

'Dennis thinks there was a train went whizzing by a few hundred years ago. Or maybe it was five minutes. Dennis has been shut in this cage so long that he gets confused. Poor old Dennis.'

'Oh, do stop saying that,' complained Jody, 'and help me find Mr Majeika and the others. At least,' she added rather doubtfully, 'do help me if you're a good dragon. If you're a bad one, I'd rather not have anything to do with you.'

The dragon thought for a few moments. 'Dennis used to be a good

dragon, when he had his freedom. He
never burnt farmers' crops, and he only
used to singe the beards of really wicked
wizards. He once tried to singe the beard
of a horrid witch called Wilhelmina
Worlock, but she didn't have a beard,
and he set her hat on fire instead, which
made her so cross, she shut him in this
cage. Poor old Dennis.' At this, the
dragon started to cry.

Jody thought about this. 'Was Miss
Worlock strong enough to do that?' she
asked. 'You're a very big dragon. Surely
she couldn't overpower you?'

At this, the dragon sobbed even
louder. 'Dennis was silly. He'd forgotten
to stoke up with coal that day. He'd gone
out in the morning, after only having
two tiny lumps for breakfast, and it soon
burnt up, and his fire went out. And
when a dragon's fire goes out, any old

wizard or witch can put spells on him, and lock him up in a horrid cage, like Madam did to Dennis after he'd set her hat on fire. Poor old Dennis.'

'It's her you call Madam?' Jody asked. 'Because she's your boss now?'

The dragon nodded. 'If Dennis calls her Madam, she might like him more, and maybe let him out one day, in a few hundred years' time. That's what Madam says. But Dennis doesn't really think she will. Poor old Dennis.' He was now weeping buckets.

'Supposing I found you some coal,' said Jody. 'Would that cheer you up?'

The dragon's eyes popped open wide, and he stopped crying. 'Would that cheer Dennis up? That would do wonders for him. Even a couple of lumps of coal, and Dennis would be able to fly again, a little.'

56

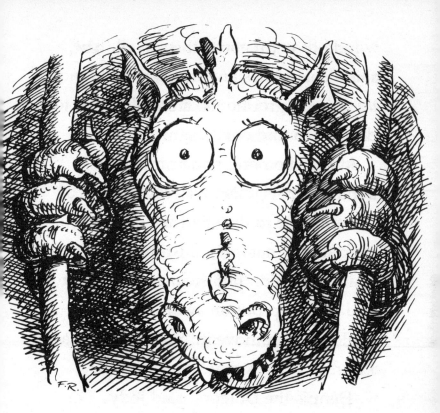

'And magic himself – I mean, yourself
– out of the cage?' asked Jody. 'And find
Miss Worlock, and stop her doing harm
to Mr Majeika and all my friends?'

The dragon nodded. 'Dennis thinks he
could easily do that. But where would
she find the coal? Dennis doesn't know
where they keep the coal down here.'

Jody thought about this. 'Well,' she said, 'coal-mines are underground, and *we're* underground, so it shouldn't be too difficult to find one.'

At this moment, she heard steps behind her. Hamish was coming out of the entrance to the staircase. He still looked very nervous. 'I t-t-tried to go up again,' he said, 'but the manhole cover had been p-p-put on again, and I couldn't m-m-move it.' Suddenly he saw Dennis. 'What's that?' he shrieked.

'Dennis the Dragon,' said Jody. 'Dennis, meet Hamish Bigmore.'

Dennis took a look at Hamish. 'Dennis doesn't think the Hamish looks very nice,' he said. 'Dennis thinks the Hamish is the sort of creature that would poke a nasty stick in Dennis's eye when he was asleep. Poor old Dennis.'

'You bet I would,' said Hamish. 'What

a horrid mangy old thing you are. I'm glad someone's shut you in a cage.'

Dennis tried to roar angrily at Hamish, but all that would come out was a sort of gasp. 'Poor old Dennis,' muttered the dragon to itself for the umpteenth time, and started to cry again.

'Oh, stop it, you two,' said Jody.

'Dennis, stop feeling sorry for yourself, and Hamish, have some sense. If we can find some coal to get the dragon's fire going, he'll be the most powerful creature you've ever seen.'

'That old thing?' mocked Hamish. 'He looks like a collapsed handbag.'

'You'll be amazed what he can do when his fire lights up again,' said Jody, hoping she was right. 'He'll be more powerful than any witch or wizard. He can do absolutely anything.'

'Really?' said Hamish nastily, beginning to get interested. 'In that case, he could help to make me ruler of the world. C'mon then, what are we wasting time for? Let's find him some coal.'

6.   *No more spells*

'Come on, Mr Majeika!' called Pete. 'Do some spells to stop stupid old Miss Worlock from shutting us up here for ever and ever!'

'Yes,' shouted the rest of Class Three. 'Come on, Mr Majeika!'

Mr Majeika thought for a moment. It was a long time since he had had a battle of spells with Wilhelmina, and he was very out of practice. It would be easy to make a mistake in the heat of the moment, and turn himself into something that she could easily hurt or kill. As for casting a spell over *her*, a powerful witch who practised her spells daily, that was something Mr Majeika knew he couldn't bring off without a lot of planning.

He decided to repeat a trick he'd once played before – turning himself into a flea, which would bite her all over. He tried to remember the spell for doing this. He knew it came in the section of his spell book which had spells for making yourself a lot smaller, and also a lot bigger. He tried to remember the words, then said them quickly under his breath.

Oh dear! It must have been the wrong spell, because he felt himself blowing up like a balloon. Yes, that was it, on the page opposite the flea spell was one which did exactly that, turned you into a gigantic balloon. And now it was too late to stop!

Class Three watched in horror as Mr Majeika got bigger and bigger, and rounder and rounder, and began to float in the air.

'Tee-hee!' cackled Miss Worlock. 'Silly old Majeika has made a bit of a mistake, hasn't he? Now, let me see if I can find a pin.'

'Oh no!' shouted Thomas. 'If she sticks a pin into him, he'll go bang, and that'll be the end of Mr Majeika. Oh, come on, Mr Majeika, can't you rescue yourself?'

Mr Majeika could hear Thomas, but he had made the mistake of turning himself into a thing, rather than an animal or person, and things can't talk, or say spells – not without a huge effort. And Mr Majeika suddenly felt very tired. The whizzing round of the Ghost Train when it first set off had quite upset his stomach, and now he was feeling terribly bloated on account of being a balloon. He tried to speak, but no words would come out. And without words, he couldn't say a spell.

'Well, well,' gloated Wilhelmina Worlock. 'No more spells from silly old Majeika! I'll tell you what, dearies, I won't puncture him with this pin *if you behave yourselves*! You must all be good little kiddiwinks and run the Weather Factory for Wilhelmina for the rest of your lives, or else I'll stick this pin into stupid Majeika, and bang! That'll be the end of him. Now, get on with it!'

'Wait a minute, Miss Worlock,' said Pete. 'Why are you in charge of this Weather Factory? What's it got to do with you?'

'A good question,' said the weather man, who was just putting on his coat before leaving. '*She*'s supposed to be the one who runs it. She was sent down here as a punishment for being a particularly nasty witch, and she was supposed to spend the rest of her life – about ten thousand years – working all the weather machines. But she tricked me into doing the job for her. She put an advertisement in the newspaper, it said: "Do you want lots of sunshine on your holiday? Then we have just the place for you to go." Well, there is lots of sunshine. But there's lots of every other kind of weather as well. And it's ten years since she put a spell on me to imprison me here.'

'Be off with you!' hissed Wilhelmina to the weather man, 'or I won't take the spell off you, and you can stay here for ever and ever with the others. Now, the rest of you, get on with it!'

Meanwhile, a long long way Upstairs, Mr Potter was looking out of the window

of his office. The weather had been
murky all morning, but now the sun had
come out. That was good, because he
was supposed to be taking Class Two for
PE. He went down to their classroom,
and told them all to come out into the
playground.

As they followed him outside, there
was a sudden clap of thunder, and
everyone screamed. Then there was a
flash of lightning – *after* the thunder,
which Mr Potter thought was very odd.
Then it began to snow, which Mr Potter
thought even odder. But he had no
sooner ordered Class Two indoors again
when an enormous rainbow appeared,
and the sun came out. And then,
suddenly, there was thick fog . . .

Downstairs, far far below St Barty's
School, Class Three were pulling every
lever in sight. Wilhelmina Worlock had
gone off, leaving them to run the
Weather Factory, and telling them to
behave themselves, otherwise she would
put a particularly nasty spell on them. As
soon as she was out of sight, Pete said:
'Let's make the maddest weather we
possibly can. Then everyone Upstairs

will notice that something is wrong, and they'll send down a search party to rescue us.'

So they tried it. But time passed, and no rescue party came.

'The trouble is,' said Thomas, 'that the weather Upstairs is always odd. It's always raining or snowing when you least expect it. So they won't notice the difference.'

'And supposing they did know we were down here,' said Pandora, 'they might want us to stay here, so they could tell us what weather they wanted on special days and at special times. They might even pay us to give them fine weather for the school sports day, and things like that. We could get rich!'

'That's the sort of idea Hamish Bigmore would think of,' said Pete. 'I wonder where he is. And where Jody is. Do you know, Mr Majeika?'

They kept talking to Mr Majeika all the time, in the hope that it would stop him being a balloon. But he just hung there silently in the middle of the Weather Factory, looking miserable.

At first, everyone quite enjoyed themselves, pulling all the handles to make the various kinds of weather happen. But then two things started to go wrong. First, their wellington boots gradually melted, as Mr Majeika's spell wore off, and they didn't turn back into shoes, so everyone found they were standing in their stockinged feet. And the floor of the Weather Factory was cold and wet, with all the fog and frost that was flying about the place, so soon they were all shivering.

The second thing was that they started to get hungry. It was hours since they

had had breakfast, and there seemed to
be nothing to eat in the place. 'What did
the weather man find to eat, I wonder?'
said Pandora.

'Maybe he didn't eat at all,' said
Thomas. 'If Wilhelmina Worlock had put
a spell on him, it's possible that he

71

simply didn't need food. But no one has put a spell on us, and we certainly do! We can't live off mouthfuls of fog.'

At that moment, there was a timid knock on the door of the Weather Factory. Class Three had discovered that they couldn't go outside because Wilhelmina had put some sort of invisible barrier in the doorway, to stop them escaping, but they were able to open the door. Pete opened it now.

'Hello,' said Jody, who was standing outside. 'I'm glad I've found you all. This is Dennis the Dragon.'

7. Wilhelmina has a bit of trouble

Everyone crowded round the doorway to look at the dragon. 'He doesn't look very strong,' said Thomas, peering at the sad bundle of wings and tail, and the miserable-looking head.

'He's not,' said Jody. 'He ran out of coal ages and ages ago – Miss Worlock starved him of it – and without coal, a dragon just fades away. But Hamish has gone to look for some, and Dennis (that's his name) is much better already, just because he's been thinking about the chances of having a mouthful of coal in an hour or two. Isn't that right, Dennis?'

'Dennis is very, very hungry,' said the dragon mournfully. 'He's trying to remember what coal tastes like. Poor

Dennis. Poor, poor Dennis.' The dragon
crumpled up even more, and looked half
dead.

'Now, Dennis, don't behave like that,'
said Jody sternly. 'You were doing fine a
few minutes ago. You managed to melt the
bars of your cage, so there must be a bit of
fire left in your tummy still.' Jody felt for

74

the invisible barrier, put up by Wilhelmina Worlock, which made it impossible to get through the door of the Weather Factory. 'Come on, Dennis,' she said, 'see what you can do with this. Just think flames! That's what worked last time.'

The dragon screwed up his eyes and thought hard. After a moment, there was a low rumbling in his belly, and an instant later smoke began to trickle out of his nostrils. With difficulty, he reared himself up to his full height, and with a roar opened his mouth. Out darted a flame! It licked around the invisible barrier; there was a hissing sound and a lot of black smoke.

Jody reached out in front of her. The invisible barrier had gone. 'Hooray!' she shouted. 'Well done, Dennis! Now everyone can escape.'

'Come and look round the Weather

Factory before we go,' said Thomas. 'It's
worth seeing. Besides, shouldn't you be
waiting for Hamish Bigmore to bring the
coal?'

'I can't think why you're trusting
Hamish to help with the plan,' said Pete.
'Why didn't you fetch the coal yourself?'

'I was in a hurry,' said Jody. 'I needed
to find you, to make sure you were all

76

right. And I think Hamish will be sensible for once. He seemed as keen to get Dennis's fire going again as I was.'

'Knowing Hamish,' said Pandora, 'he's probably got some nasty plan of his own up his sleeve. But Jody, look what happened to Mr Majeika!' She pointed at the balloon, which was looking more miserable than ever.

'Oh no!' exclaimed Jody. 'Can't he turn himself back again?' They explained to her what had happened. 'I wonder,' said Jody thoughtfully. 'Dennis has been telling me that dragons are much more powerful magicians than witches and wizards. Dennis, could you turn Mr Majeika back into himself?'

'Dennis will have to think about it,' said the dragon, who seemed to be exhausted after melting the invisible barrier. 'If only he had his coal . . . Hark!

Dennis hears someone coming. Could it be the coal-bringer, at last?'

Jody peered out of the door. 'It is!' she said excitedly. 'Hamish is pushing a big barrow full of coal. But there's somebody riding on it. Oh no! It's –

She didn't need to finish, because they could all hear a well-known voice cackling away. 'Tee hee! Hurry up, my Star Pupil, and then we can catch this fine dragon you've been telling me about, and use it for our wicked plan. Faster, faster!'

'Quick, Dennis,' said Jody, 'hide behind this fog machine. Then we can pretend you're not here.'

'Dennis doesn't like fog,' grumbled the dragon. 'It makes his fire go out.' But he waddled over to a corner of the Weather Factory, and hid behind the large grey machine which made the fog.

He had hidden not a moment too
soon. There in the doorway, stood
Wilhelmina and her Star Pupil. Hamish
was covered in black smudges. 'Did you
enjoy being a coal-miner, Hamish?'
asked Thomas, laughing.

Hamish glared at him. 'Your laughing
days are over. From now on, we're in

charge! Mr Majeika doesn't stand a chance! How do you like being a balloon, silly old Mr Majeika?' He stuck his tongue out at the balloon.

And the balloon stuck its tongue out at Hamish.

Everyone gasped, and Miss Worlock began to look worried. 'Who's meddling with spells?' she muttered. 'Majeika shouldn't be able to do that.'

'Well, I can, Wilhelmina,' said the balloon, 'because there's somebody here whose magic is more powerful than yours. Here we go!' And, shouting these words, Mr Majeika suddenly turned back into himself again.

Everyone cheered. 'Well done, Dennis,' called Mr Majeika, and the dragon came crawling out from behind the fog machine. 'Your magic is far more powerful than silly old Wilhelmina's.

She's completely in your power, isn't
she?'

'Dennis is certainly feeling a lot better,'
said the dragon, looking pleased with
himself. 'But he'd be even stronger if he
had a mouthful of that coal.' He looked
greedily at the wheelbarrow.

'And Dennis can have all the coal in

the world,' said Miss Worlock, 'if he comes with me and my Star Pupil.' The dragon licked its lips hungrily, as Miss Worlock picked a big lump of coal out of the barrow, and held it out to him. 'Yes, Dennis, all the coal you can eat, if you'll fly Upstairs with me and my Star Pupil on your back.' The dragon licked its lips again, and then nodded.

'What are you going to do when you get there?' said Jody nervously.

'Why, make things very nasty indeed for people who won't do what we tell them,' said Miss Worlock, with a horrible grin. 'It's not very nice having a dragon land on your roof-top and set your house, or your palace, or your government buildings, on fire. And that's what we're going to do to anyone who doesn't obey our orders, aren't we, my Star Pupil?'

'You bet we are,' said Hamish. 'Over here, Dennis.' Hamish held out more lumps of coal, but there was no need to lure the dragon over. He was already making a rush at the wheelbarrow, and in a moment he had gobbled up every single lump of coal. 'That's right,' said Hamish. 'And there's lots more where that came from.'

Everyone could hear the roaring of the

fire in Dennis's tummy now, and he seemed to grow to twice his size as he stood up properly on his back legs for the first time, and began to flap his gigantic wings.

Hamish and Wilhelmina climbed on to the dragon's back, and held on tight.

Black smoke and steam billowed from his nostrils, as he took to the air, and carried Hamish and Miss Worlock out of the door of the Weather Factory, and away into the distance.

'This is terrible, Mr Majeika,' said Jody. 'I didn't think Dennis would let us down like this.'

'He hasn't,' said Mr Majeika. 'Before he flew off, he gave me a great big wink. So I reckon he's still on our side.'

'I didn't see him wink,' said Pete. 'I was watching his face the whole time, and he never even moved his eyelids.'

'Dragons don't wink with their eyelids,' said Mr Majeika. 'They flap one of their wings in a certain way that every wizard and witch recognizes. That's to say, every wizard and witch who really knows about dragons. Obviously Wilhelmina doesn't. So she may have a nasty surprise in store!'

8. *Hamish gets a job*

'The weather seems to be getting better now,' said Mr Potter to the weather man. (He had arrived at St Barty's School just after lunch and had been given a job as a science teacher, since he said he knew a lot about weather.) They took a stroll together across the playground. It was rather quiet without Class Three, who had been away all day, but Mr Potter had learnt not to worry when that sort of thing happened. For some reason, Mr Majeika's class were always disappearing, but since they always came back in the end, looking as if they'd had a good time, it didn't bother him.

'Yes, it's quite a nice day,' said the weather man, who was worried, because he knew that Class Three and Mr

Majeika had been trapped in the Weather
Factory by Miss Worlock. But he didn't
like to tell Mr Potter. He just hoped that
they would somehow escape.

'Wait a minute,' said Mr Potter.
'What's that? It seems to be a very
strange aeroplane. And it's on fire!'

Something with flapping wings was
approaching at high speed, with steam

and smoke, and even flames, pouring out of the front. Two people were sitting on the back of it, cackling with horrid laughter. 'I think it's a dragon,' said the weather man.

Mr Potter scratched his head. He thought the new teacher had said 'dragon', and that was certainly what the thing looked like. And the people on the back of it closely resembled Hamish Bigmore and some old woman whom Mr Potter thought he had seen somewhere before. They were cackling like mad, and shouting: 'We're going to rule the world. Watch out, St Barty's, here we come!'

The dragon was flying over the school now, and suddenly the shouts of its two passengers changed to screams. The dragon had dropped them! Down they fell, straight into the big rubbish bin where the school cook and the dinner-

ladies tipped all the nasty leftovers from lunch. 'Yuck!' shouted Hamish and Miss Worlock.

'Dennis has had enough of you two!' called the dragon. 'He's going to find a nice coal-mine, and he'll spend the rest of his days there in comfort. Goodbye!' And as he said this last word, he let out a great roar of flame, which caught the edge of the school bicycle shed, and set it on fire.

It was at this moment that a manhole cover in the middle of the playground opened, and Mr Majeika peered out. 'Oh, good,' he said. 'I've taken the right short cut. We're back, everyone.' He climbed out, and the rest of Class Three followed him.

'Good afternoon, Mr Potter,' they all said.

'Hello, there,' said Mr Potter, scratching his head. 'Been on another trip, have you?'

It was three weeks later, and everyone had almost forgotten about the strange adventure underground. Miss Worlock wouldn't bother them again for some time to come. 'She made a dreadful mistake sitting on the dragon's back,' explained Mr Majeika. 'A wizard or witch must never touch a dragon. If they do, all their magic power drains out of them, and won't come back for ages and ages.' Mr Majeika had used his own magic to banish Wilhelmina back to the Weather Factory, where she was supposed to be, and he had set her to work making the weather.

Dennis the Dragon had found a nice coal-mine, but had soon become bored. He sent Mr Majeika a letter asking if a job could be found for him in Adventure Galaxy. 'Dennis could give the children a really good ride,' he wrote.

'That's a good idea,' said Mr Majeika. 'We'll ask the people at Adventure Galaxy, when we all go there on Saturday to see Hamish Bigmore doing his new job.'

Mr Potter had told Hamish he must pay for the bike shed to be rebuilt, so Hamish had had to find a Saturday job to get some money. He boasted to everyone that he had found a very good one at Adventure Galaxy, but he wouldn't say what it was. 'I'm the most important person in the whole place,' was all he would say.

On Saturday, the whole of Class Three went to Adventure Galaxy with Mr Majeika. They couldn't see Hamish anywhere. He wasn't on the gate taking the money; he wasn't in charge of any of the rides; he wasn't selling ice-cream or coke or candy floss. At last they gave up. 'I don't think Hamish is working here at all,' said Thomas. 'I bet he's just doing a paper round or something. Come on, let's go home.'

It was then that they saw the new

Ghost Train. It was smart and shiny, and had a big tent behind the front of it, and an ordinary-looking person was showing people to their seats. 'I don't *think* this is another of Wilhelmina's tricks,' said Mr Majeika. 'Come on, everyone, let's have a ride before we go home.'

They climbed aboard the train, a hooter sounded, and off they went into the darkness. It was all rather disappointing compared to the ride they'd had last time. There were painted ghost-shapes, and mirrors, and one or two laser effects, but nothing very exciting until they were near the end of the ride. Then suddenly, a skeleton leapt out at them from the darkness, crying 'Boo!'

Some of Class Three jumped and screamed, but Jody said: 'I know that voice!' She poked a finger in the skeleton's ribs.

'Get off, Jody!' yelped the skeleton.
'Leave me alone!'

'So that's Hamish's Saturday job,' said
Mr Majeika. 'Well, I must say Hamish
Bigmore is a good deal nastier than
anything we saw on the real Ghost
Train!'

Read more in Puffin

For complete information about books available from Puffin – and Penguin – and how to order them, contact us at the appropriate address below. Please note that for copyright reasons the selection of books varies from country to country.

www.puffin.co.uk

In the United Kingdom: Please write to Dept EP, Penguin Books Ltd,
Bath Road, Harmondsworth, West Drayton, Middlesex UB7 ODA

In the United States: Please write to Penguin Group (USA), Inc., P.O. Box 12289,
Dept B, Newark, New Jersey 07101–5289 or call 1–800–788–6262

In Canada: Please write to Penguin Books Canada Ltd,
10 Alcorn Avenue, Suite 300, Toronto, Ontario M4V 3B2

In Australia: Please write to Penguin Books Australia Ltd,
250 Camberwell Road, Camberwell, Victoria 3124

In New Zealand: Please write to Penguin Books (NZ) Ltd,
Private Bag 102902, North Shore Mail Centre, Auckland 10

In India: Please write to Penguin Books India Pvt Ltd,
11 Panscheel Shopping Centre, Panscheel Park, New Delhi 110 017

In the Netherlands: Please write to Penguin Books Netherlands bv,
Postbus 3507, NL–1001 AH Amsterdam

In Germany: Please write to Penguin Books Deutschland GmbH,
Metzlerstrasse 26, 60594 Frankfurt am Main

In Spain: Please write to Penguin Books S. A., Bravo Murillo 19,
1° B, 28015 Madrid

In Italy: Please write to Penguin Italia s.r.l.,
Via Felice Casati 20, I–20124 Milano

In France: Please write to Penguin France S. A.,
17 rue Lejeune, F–31000 Toulouse

In Japan: Please write to Penguin Books Japan, Ishikiribashi Building,
2–5–4, Suido, Bunkyo-ku, Tokyo 112

In South Africa: Please write to Longman Penguin Southern Africa (Pty) Ltd,
Private Bag X08, Bertsham 2013